TINY TIM

DOG DIARIES

DOG DIARIES

SPECIAL EDITION

TINY TIM

BY KATE KLIMO • ILLUSTRATED BY TIM JESSELL

RANDOM HOUSE 🏠 NEW YORK

Text copyright © 2017 by Kate Klimo
Cover art and interior illustrations copyright © 2017 by Tim Jessell
Photographs courtesy of Museum of Fine Arts, Boston, p.ix; Time Life Pictures/The LIFE Picture Collection/Getty Images, p.143; Hans Surfer/Moment/Getty Images, p.148

Visit us on the Web! randomhousekids.com

Educators and librarians, for a variety of teaching tools, visit us at
RHTeachersLibrarians.com

Library of Congress Cataloging-in-Publication Data
Names: Klimo, Kate, author. | Jessell, Tim, illustrator.
Title: Tiny Tim / by Kate Klimo ; illustrated by Tim Jessell.
Description: First edition. | New York : Random House, [2017] | Series: Dog diaries ; 11 |
Summary: "Charles Dickens's dog Timber tells the story of his life with the great writer."—
Provided by publisher.
Identifiers: LCCN 2016035108 (print) | LCCN 2017007021 (ebook) |
ISBN 978-0-399-55131-4 (trade pbk.) | ISBN 978-0-399-55132-1 (lib. bdg.) |
ISBN 978-0-399-55133-8 (ebook)
Subjects: | CYAC: Havanese dog—Fiction. | Dogs—Fiction. | Human-animal relationships—
Fiction. | Dickens, Charles, 1812–1870—Fiction.
Classification: LCC PZ10.3.K686 Ti 2017 (print) | LCC PZ10.3.K686 (ebook) |
DDC [Fic]—dc23

Printed in the United States of America

10 9 8 7 6 5 4 3 2

First Edition

For Charlie Kolster, a fine figure of a man
—K.K.

For those who are not like Mr. Scrooge—
they have a dog.
—T.J.

CONTENTS

This portrait of Charles Dickens was painted by Francis Alexander in 1842, during the author's first American tour, on which he acquired Timber.

I Am Born

Whether I shall turn out to be the hero of my own life, or whether some other dog will hold that role, these pages will show. I record that I was born in the year 1841 in a corner of the Baltimore dressing room of an Actor. As fate would have it, he had Great Plans for me.

After watching my brother, Carlos, and sister, Blanca, spirited off in the arms of doting strangers,

I fell into a funk. Was this it for me? Was I to live the rest of my life here, watching Players pace the floor and practice their lines? Or did life hold some grander purpose?

My beloved mama answered these questions one day when I was four months old.

Today, my son, the Player is giving you away as a gift to his friend Charles Dickens. Mr. Dickens is a Great Writer, she said. *This is an enormous honor.*

What is a Great Writer? I asked.

A Great Writer writes stories, which are printed up in things called books, precious objects you must never chew, however tempting and tasty you might find the paper.

I knew something of stories. I knew that the Players acted out stories onstage every night before cheering crowds. Mama told us stories, too. They were exciting tales of her journey from the faraway island of Cuba to America. They call our kind Havana Silk Dogs, after that fair city in Cuba. (Today they call us Havanese.) Only the finest Cuban families boasted of owning Silk Dogs.

You are to be the Great Writer's Companion, Mama explained.

But why me? I asked.

Because you are a splendid example of our kind. We Silk Dogs are famous not just for our fine coats, but for something else of far greater import: we possess Special Powers.

She leaned in so close to me that I felt her sweet breath stirring my whiskers. *We can read the minds of our masters!*

In the years to come, I would learn to read the mind of Charles Dickens like an open book. It was a mind as complex and fascinating as any of his stories. What I learned would make me a far better companion than some drooling hound who fetches dead birds in its maw.

Dickens arrived that evening in low spirits. He was a handsome fellow with bright, intelligent eyes and dark curls. I took an instant liking to him. The Player held me up. How fetching I looked with my white hair combed into a topknot! But sadly, Dickens's spirits were not improved by the sight of my adorable self.

"I have named him Boz," said the Player proudly. "After your very own pen name. I have bred him just for you."

I wagged my tail, eager to please.

"I am only halfway through this tour to promote my books in America. Wherever I go, I am stormed by strangers who want to shake my hand. By womenfolk who come at me with scissors to cut a lock of my hair. They even dare to snip the fur from my coat collar. Let us hope that this *ridiculous* dog will survive the ordeal."

Ridiculous, was I? My heart raced. My hackles rose. I looked up into his face and began to bark

with all my might. *Sir, you do me a grave disservice! Far from being ridiculous, I am made of sterner stuff than you know!*

Dickens tossed his head back and roared with laughter. "Isn't *he* a lively little chap? He barks, as the vulgar expression goes, like bricks!"

Having said my piece, I settled down in a huff. In the years to come, Dickens would hear much of this loud, brick-like bark. He always fancied he knew why I barked. But he never understood me quite so well as I understood him. For I am a Havana Silk Dog with Special Powers.

But my barking like bricks did the trick. Dickens thanked the Player for his kindness and bore me away with him in a basket tucked under his arm.

That night in our hotel room, I met Dickens's sweet-faced wife, Catherine Hogarth, along with her servant, Anne Brown. The Dickenses' four small children had been left at home in a place they called England.

The first thing I noticed about Catherine was that she was a clumsy creature. Just walking across the room, she would bump into tables or trip on rugs. Was it the confusion of being in a strange land with strange ways? Or did she simply not wish to be in this country? After all, she was not the writer whose fame would benefit from touring America. But I gather that Dickens had insisted she come. Rather unkindly, he called her Clumsy Kate. To me, she would always be the Poor Dear.

Early the next morning, we set out to the next destination on Dickens's book tour—the bustling city of Pittsburgh. We traveled by rail, on a long snake of iron cars pulled by a fire-breathing monster called a locomotive. Unused to the stench of the monster's breath and the constant rude jostling of its cars, I confess that I threw up the kidney pie I had eaten for breakfast. It fell to Anne Brown, bless her heart, to clean out my basket and wash my fouled fur.

"Poor little dear," she said as she smoothed my fur. "I know just how you feel. Oh, how I miss England!"

In Pittsburgh, Dickens entered crowded auditoriums, where he read aloud in a dramatic voice from his most famous books. In time, I would grow familiar with the words from *Oliver Twist* and *The Old Curiosity Shop*. Afterward, the crowds fell upon him. They wrung Dickens's hand and snipped at his hair and grabbed at his coat. Dickens handed me off to his host lest the crowd crush me.

Later, I accompanied him on a visit to a prison. In that bleak and unhappy place, the haunted souls peered out of their cages at us. *Help us!* their hollow eyes seemed to say.

This was the first of many such trips I would take in the company of the Great Writer. For him, no tour of a city was complete without a visit to its prisons, its hospitals, its madhouses, and its slums.

"The public ignores such places at their own peril, my furry little friend," he said to me.

Dickens was a man rare in his time—or any other. He was bent on improving the world. Telling stories set in such places was his way of doing this. He was also a most enthusiastic letter writer. During his tour of America, he wrote many a long letter home to friends and family in England, sharing his impressions.

In those first few days together, our attachment to each other grew. I noticed that he never called me Boz. Boz, as he explained to me, had been his pen name when first he began to write. Moses was the nickname given to his brother Augustus. When he was a wee lad, Dickens couldn't quite manage it. It came out "Boses," and that became Boz. Apparently, he did not feel Boz suited me. Instead he called me little doggy.

It was in Cincinnati, on the banks of the mighty Ohio River, that he began calling me Snittle Timbery. I cannot say I cared for the new name, which belonged to a character in one of his books, *Nicholas Nickleby*. It was a foolish-enough-sounding name for a human. For a dog it was simply silly. Still, I perked my ears and came running when he called, "Come, my Snittle Timbery!"

As we boarded a paddleboat steamer to travel down the muddy river, the Great One said to me, "Be on your guard, Snittle Timbery, lest the gulls carry you off."

I ducked low in my basket. The birds, very nearly as large as I, screeched and dived at me. Oh, but they were an upstart lot! They plucked the very food from my mouth and snatched at my curls!

Ouch! I yelped. *I say—go easy on a fellow! What have I ever done to you?*

You have fine silky fur perfect for weaving into our nests, they cackled.

Well, you can't have it. Fie on you, thieves! I barked and snapped.

The birds were but one of the dangers. The river was cluttered with logs and floating wreckage and the bodies of dead cows. I was knocked from side to side as the steamer shifted to avoid crashing into these obstacles. I had lived my life thus far in a single room whose floor never moved. So you can imagine the state of my nerves.

The Ohio River having become now the

Mississippi River, we stopped briefly at the town of Cairo. Dickens declared it "a dismal swamp."

Down in our cramped cabin, he took up his quill and wrote to a friend. "This is not the republic I came to see. . . . This is not the republic of my imagination. This is a low, coarse, and mean nation driven by a herd of rascals. Pah!"

I came to understand that his disgust with America had less to do with its cities and terrain and more to do with the reading public. You see, they did not pay Dickens for his stories. It was the fault of scoundrel newspaper editors, who published them for their own profit without paying Dickens a single cent. And when, in the halls and banquets of his tour, Dickens complained of this piracy, the crowds booed him off the stage. They wanted to be entertained, not suffer through a lecture on copyright law.

And the Poor Dear—how she suffered! The louts on board the steamer stood on deck chewing plugs of tobacco. This nasty habit was very popular among the men of America. On land, they spewed their gobs of tobacco into pots called spittoons. On the river, they simply spat them overboard. The wind would blow the slimy spittle back on deck—onto the Poor Dear's lovely frocks! By the end of the day, her skirts were fouled with yellow-brown streaks. Every night Anne Brown had to scrub them clean.

After a few days, we left the river behind us and boarded a stagecoach. I cannot say that this was much of an improvement. We traveled over roads made of logs. *Bumpety-bump-bump* all the day long. I lurched from one side of the coach to the other. I tell you, my brains rattled in my head!

"Cheer up, Timbery," Dickens said. "You're

about to look upon one of Nature's Wonders."

Is that a fact? I seethed.

When we arrived at the Falls of Niagara, my brick-like bark was cut short by the thunder of the falling water. I stood and watched Nature's Wonder sliding off an enormous shelf onto the rocks below. What if a small white dog were to slip and fall into these rushing waters? I shivered from nose to tail.

Much as they terrified me, these Falls were all that the Great Writer could have hoped for. This single wonder of nature made the whole trip worthwhile for him. For hours, he stood spellbound on the bank. Above the mighty pounding, he shouted, "Ah, Timbery! Do you feel it, little doggy? Do you feel how near to the Creator we are standing?"

I, for one, felt nothing but a bone-chilling cold. And wet! I shook myself until my ears rang and still I could not rid my coat of the clinging veil of dampness. When we left the mighty Niagara behind, I fell to the floor of the train car into a deep and twitching swoon.

Our train trip of several days' time ended at a ship's dock. I soon found myself aboard a seagoing vessel. A vast body of water surrounded us. There was not a speck of land in sight. For the first few days, I was in a state of panic. I ran up and down the deck.

Above me, a great gray gull wheeled and called out, *What's wrong with you, tiny fur face?*

What's wrong with me? I said. *Do you see a single tree or bush against which a dog might lift a leg?*

You're at sea, fur face. You'll just have to make do like the rest of us.

Finally, in desperation, I crouched on a coil of rope. Sweet relief!

Dear Anne Brown came after me with a bucket of seawater and washed the mess overboard, as she would throughout the voyage. After a few days, that coil of rope and I became fast friends.

Life at sea might have been a struggle for me, but I had never seen the Great One happier. He passed hours on deck playing his squeeze-box and singing "Home, Sweet Home." I lay at his feet with my nose on my paws and stared up at him, sad-eyed.

"Cheer up, little doggy. The book tour is over and done with. We'll soon be off this ship and safe on English soil. Oh, there is no place like England! You shall see it, and be happier and merrier than ever in your doggy life. I promise you that, my little man."

I Meet My Match

Happier and merrier? Perhaps a better way to put it is that I was beset with a different peril once I reached English soil.

This peril had a name. It was Grip the Second—a black bird of ill omen known as a raven. This particular raven had the run of Devonshire Terrace, Dickens's home on London's Regent's Square.

There had been a Grip the First, as well you

can imagine. He had met his maker a year before my time, having poisoned himself eating—of all things—wallpaper! I could see the spots on the wall where the paper had since been mended by some careful hand.

The dead bird now sat on the mantelshelf in the library. He was stuffed and lifeless. His black wings still shiny, his beady glass eyes stared down at me as if to say, *Look out, little dog, lest someday you become a trophy yourself.*

In years to come, Grip the First would become legendary as the bird that inspired another Great Writer—and visitor to the Dickens household— Edgar Allan Poe, to pen a famous poem called "The Raven."

Stuff and nonsense, I say. What manner of Bird could inspire a Great Writer to write anything but a Bitter Complaint to the man who had duped him into buying it in the first place?

Grip the Second let me know, the moment I set foot in the house, that Devonshire Terrace was his territory.

Be gone, vile little dishrag! he cackled at me.

Nay, I shall stay and leave . . . nevermore! said I. (I knew how to talk to a Bird of Ill Omen.)

I was dead tired from our overland trip from Liverpool. But I knew that if I did not take a stand then and there, I would be forever at his mercy. As the winged devil swooped down upon me, I reared up on my hind legs. With a sharp snap of my jaws, the house echoed with the shriek of his outrage.

A single black feather drifted to the floor at my feet.

"Oh, dear!" said the Great Writer, bending over to pick up the feather. "Grip is very proud of those tail feathers. Bad form, Timber."

From his perch atop a large vase, Grip echoed, *Bad form, Timber!*

Dickens roared with delight, which only encouraged the creature. Henceforth, the rooms of Devonshire Terrace echoed with Grip's cry, *Bad form, Timber!*

To which I would reply with a snap of my jaws, *Go eat some wallpaper!*

Hearing the commotion the two of us made, the Dickens children came tumbling out of the nursery. They kissed their dear mother and climbed all over their father, toppling him to the floor.

There were four of them, chubby and apple-cheeked. The eldest, at five, was Charles Culliford, called Charley. Then came Mary, or Mamie, aged four. Kate Macready, or Katie, was two. And little Walter Savage Landor was but a babe of one. The Poor Dear snatched Walter from his nurse's arms and covered his face with kisses. How she wept with joy!

Her tear-filled eyes met mine and seemed to say, *See? Now I am happy. At home with my children, I am truly happy.*

Having exhausted their affections on their father, the three older children now turned their attention to me.

"His name is Timber," said the Great One proudly.

"What a tiny little thing he is!" said Mamie. "Shall we call him *Tiny* Timber?"

"Capital idea! He looks like a toy! Can we play with him, Father?" Charley asked.

"Tiny Tim is MINE!" said Katie. She toddled over and grabbed a fistful of my tresses.

Gently, little one, I warned her with a low growl.

Bad form, Timber! Grip scolded.

Everyone laughed.

"No, dear children," Dickens told them, rescuing me from their sticky mitts. "Timber shall remain with me. I will allow him to visit you from time to time, but make no mistake, Timber is MINE!"

Later that night, I went with Charles for his nightly visit with the children. And a more touching scene I never saw. The Great Writer got down on all fours and allowed Katie to tack him up in single harness and ride him all over the nursery. What an absurd yet touching sight!

Then, sitting in a chair, with a child on each knee and Charley clinging to his neck, he told hair-raising tales of his trip to America. Although I had been there at his side, still I listened, rapt, to his telling. That's the kind of storyteller he was.

Afterward, they demanded that he sing to them. He sang many a silly song. One was about an old man who caught a cold while on an omnibus and got "rheumatiz" and a stiff neck. Dickens rose up

and staggered about, acting out the old man's aches and pains with all the skill of a Player. The children laughed themselves silly.

"Children! Children!" said the nurse. "It is time to settle down and sleep."

She all but shooed the Great Writer and myself from the nursery. We could still hear giggling behind the closed door.

The next day, my life with the Great Writer began in earnest. The man held himself to a strict routine. He rose at seven, breakfasted at eight, and wrote from nine in the morning until two in the afternoon. My Special Powers soon told me that the man wrote not so much for the joy of it but to make money to feed and clothe and house his family. All the time he had been in America, he was away from his writing. Now money was in short supply, and he was desperate. I did my best to comfort him, but even then I knew there was but one cure for this ill. And that was to write a Big Book and make a nice heap of money.

Let me pause here to explain to you how the Great One worked on these Big Books of his. They were lengthy stories, but they were not sold, as books are today, in one big volume. Instead, one or two chapters were sold at a time in skinny little pamphlets. Each month, a new pamphlet was published until the entire story had been told. This way, upon finishing each month's installment, readers waited in suspense for the next chapter to come out. And although Mr. Dickens had planned the entire story in advance, he wrote out the chapters only one month ahead of the readers receiving them. It was a nerve-racking business for everyone.

He had written many Big Books before I entered his life. And he would write many after I left it. But I hold a special fondness for those I sat at his feet and watched him write. The Big Book he was fixing to write now was called *Martin Chuzzlewit.*

How is that silliness? It sounded more like a sneeze than a name. I lay on the floor and watched as Dickens fretted at his desk over *Martin Chuzzlewit.* He paced. He gazed out the window. He drew doodles on a sheet of paper. He smote his head and tore at his hair. Occasionally, he would dip the tip of his goose quill into a pot of blue ink and scratch at the paper.

It was at this time that I discovered my own love of paper. You will recall that my dear mother had warned me off chewing books. But she never forbade the munching or scratching of sheets of paper. Just as Dickens liked to scratch words upon paper with a quill, so did I like to scratch paper with my claws. How I loved to hear it crackle and rip. I even licked it with my tongue. It was an activity that amused all my senses.

Alas, it was an amusement that was short-lived. Paper was an expensive item. Dickens was very particular about his paper and bought it at a special shop. When he caught me savaging a precious sheet of it, he whopped me soundly.

I ran into a corner and sulked. But, remembering the whop, I never again touched a sheet of his paper. I only stared at it in longing. I had to content myself with the sweet sound of his quill scratching word after word upon it.

Whether he was able to eke out many words or none at all, Dickens remained in the library all morning. He emerged midday for a bite to eat. I sat at his feet and accepted whatever fell my way. Then it was back to the library. Sometimes, when no words came, he would teach me tricks. He taught me to run into a corner and stand on two legs. He taught me to sit and lie down and roll over and spin around and chase my tail.

At two o'clock promptly, work ended, and we were free. It was time for our long walk through the streets of London. For a small dog, I am a good walker. And Dickens was every bit as great a walker as he was a writer. I tell you, the man could walk ten miles a day without batting an eye. On our walks, I came to know and love the streets as well as my master did. I knew its alleys and courts, lodging houses and hovels, workhouses and prisons, police offices and rag shops. Street urchins and omnibus conductors alike knew the Great Writer by sight and called out to him.

"Working on a new one, Mr. Dickens?" they would ask.

His readers were everywhere, calling to him with fond familiarity. And yet he seemed to look right through them. His mind was elsewhere. His lips moved steadily, silently, as he told himself, in dribs and drabs, the story he had in mind. And his readers understood.

You would think, with the man being so busy and beset, that he would not have had a moment to spare for my affairs. But such was not the case. He was convinced that I needed to make a brilliant and fruitful match. The man simply doted on babies—and baby dogs were no exception.

That first year, in 1842, we summered in Broadstairs, where Dickens taught me to jump over a stick at his command. How pleased he was when I caught on as quickly as I did. Didn't he know that I would have done anything for him? But I did not always bask in the warmth of his approval. There came a time when he would grow to be quite vexed with me.

In the spring of 1843, the family rented a farmhouse in Finchley. It was there that the Master got it into his head that he wished me to sire some puppies. Having discovered that the postman's dog was of my own distinguished breed, the two of us were brought together. The much-hoped-for union did not take place. The dog had no interest in me, and frankly, I had little in her.

Thoroughly disgusted with me, the Great Writer banished me to my basket on top of his bookcase and said no more about it.

I thought that was the end of it, but not six months later, I was introduced to the groom Thomas Thompson's little dog. "She's uncommon nice," the Master said, pushing me toward her.

But she was cold and standoffish, backing

herself up into a corner and snarling.

Stay away from me, she all but spat.

I beg your pardon? I was shocked, I tell you. Here I was, a gentle dog of breeding, offering my friendship. And what did she do? She put her pretty nose up in the air.

You're one of those dull-witted Fancy Dogs. I prefer the Rough and Ready types who live by their wits on the street.

Well! There was no accounting for taste. Still, I pled my case. *I assure you, my wits are quite sharp, for I spend many an hour in the company of the Great Writer. If you would but give me a chance,* I begged. I knew how badly Dickens wanted pups, and I was desperate to please him. *I'm sure you would find me a most agreeable mate.*

Every time I drew close, the slippery little creature cut and ran!

After several days, I gave up. Mr. Thompson came and took his little dog away.

Dickens was thoroughly disgusted. He could barely bring himself to look at me. He blamed me for the failure of the match.

"Charmless little lout," he muttered.

I tell you, she was a cold and wicked wench! I yelped pitifully, but he would not hear it. Instead, he turned away from me.

I hung my head.

Once again, his approval shone upon me like the rays of the sun. But apparently, Dickens had not given up on his dreams of puppy litters.

In all my life, I never did sire a single pup. You might say that I was busy answering to what was perhaps a more noble calling. I was serving as the canine companion to a Great Writer.

THE LITTLE CHRISTMAS BOOK

The writing had begun in earnest. The quill scratched away as the Great Writer sat in the library and poured out the story of one *Martin Chuzzlewit.* But something was wrong. As the chapters made their monthly appearance, I sensed they were not selling as well as those of his previous Big Books.

Dickens was beside himself. Life in London was costly. He had a good many bills to pay. What was more, the Poor Dear was expecting a fifth child.

And it wasn't just his immediate family he had to worry about. His parents and his brothers and sisters depended on him as well. His beloved sister Fanny was far from well-off. And she had a son, Harry, with a crippling disease.

Dickens paced his library, mentally tallying up his expenses.

"Timber, my little doggy," he concluded, "I must earn some ready money."

But first, inspiration was needed. That autumn, through mist and fog and frost, wrapped in greatcoat and muffler, Dickens walked the streets of London. And there was I, faithful companion, trotting at his heels. As his feet moved, so did the master's lips, silently beginning to tell a new story to himself.

This would not be just any story. It would be

the story that would take care of all his financial woes. He would need to write it quickly so that it might not take too much time away from the monthly additions to *Chuzzlewit.*

We threaded our way through the tangle of traffic, past the vendors and mongers, past the carts and drays and omnibuses. Once, we found ourselves down by the docks. In a dark alley, a gang of stray dogs surrounded us. My heart beating wildly, I held myself very still as they sniffed me up and down. I was right to be nervous. These were some rough-looking customers.

What do you reckon it is, Blackie? one of them asked the ragged spaniel who was their leader.

It's one of them gentleman's dogs, said Blackie with a scornful curl of his lip.

Is it really? another dog asked. *And here I was thinking it was a lady's muff, what with those silky curls. Pretty enough to decorate a lady's lap, ain't it now?*

You are wondering perhaps why I did not speak up and defend myself. I was outnumbered for one thing. And for another, I was lacking in experience. I had never so much as argued with another dog over a bone. I had never huddled in the ashes of a dying fire to keep the cold at bay. I had never lost the tip of my tail, as Blackie clearly had, in a back-alley brawl over turf.

In short, I was out of my element.

Dickens was as well, to be sure. But was he afraid? Not a bit! He poked his walking stick at them. "Run along, good fellows, and be about your business. There is nothing for you here."

And—just like that!—they scattered. Such was the power, in those days, of a gentleman's walking stick.

I have told you earlier of Dickens's interest in prisons and workhouses and hospitals. At this time, he began to take an interest in schools. The children of the wealthy were spared no expense in their education. For the poor, there were only the so-called Ragged Schools. We visited together one such place. It was three shabby rooms on the first floor of a rotten house. The children, dressed in rags, received lessons that were deadly dull and hardly worth the learning.

Afterward, Dickens muttered darkly in my ear, "These children deserve better, Timber."

I growled low in a show of agreement.

"Ignorance is the cause of society's ills, my fine, furry friend. Therefore, education is the means to cure it."

This would be the message of his new story. And the best time to publish such a story, he claimed, was at Christmas.

"You know, Tim," he told me one day as he warmed to his new theme, "Christmas is a good time, a forgiving, charitable, pleasant time; the only time I know of in the long calendar of the year when men and women seem to open their shut-up hearts freely and to think of people below them as if they really were fellow passengers and not another race of creatures."

He finally sat down one chill October morn

and started to write. His story needed to be finished to go on sale that very Christmas. Urgency was the order of the day. And so the Great Writer wrote, you should excuse the expression, as if a pack of dockside dogs were nipping at his heels.

I watched in fascination as he scratched away. Now and then, I saw him leap up from his chair like a scalded cat. He would dash over to the mirror and make faces, speaking in strange and different voices. This is what I heard him say:

The first voice, being young and robust and cheery, said, "A merry Christmas, uncle Scrooge! God save you!"

Then his face seemed to wither with age. "Bah! Humbug!" he answered in a voice as hard as flint.

The cheerful voice came back: "Christmas a humbug, uncle! You don't mean that, I am sure?"

The flinty voice replied: "I do. Merry Christmas! What right have you to be merry? What reason have you to be merry? You're poor enough."

To which the cheery voice came right back: "Come, then. What right have you to be dismal? What reason have you to be morose? You're rich enough."

Then, in his own voice, Dickens would cry, "That's it!" And run back to his desk for another round of furious scribbling.

This is how he created the story over a period of six weeks. As a Player first, acting it out for himself (and me), then as a writer, setting it down on paper for others to read.

After I recovered from my fear of the strange voices and faces, I came to enjoy the process. I looked forward each day to meeting new voices and faces. The most memorable of these belonged to a character named Ebenezer Scrooge, who was given to the expression "Bah, humbug!"

Bah, humbug, indeed! What a jolly good story.

On the day he finished the story and wrote "The End," underslashed twice, a new kind of work began. He personally chose the printing paper, the ink, and the rose-colored cloth for the cover of the new book. He personally chose the illustrator and supervised the illustrations. Then he delivered both words and pictures to the printer for making into a beautiful little book.

While the book was being made, he was more nervous than a fox in a kennel. He paced about the house. He fidgeted and fretted. "I hope to get a great deal of money out of this idea," he told a friend.

As Christmas neared, Charles read the story aloud at dinner parties all over town. Everyone who heard it delighted in it. He gave early copies to his friends. From the paper to the ink to the binding to the words on the page, how proud he was of every aspect of it!

On December 17, only eight days before

Christmas, the book went on sale. No longer was it called *The Little Christmas Book*. For a short book, it had a rather long title. It was *A Christmas Carol, in Prose: Being a Ghost Story of Christmas.*

As the Great Writer waited to hear whether the public would like it, the whole household seemed to be holding its breath. Even Grip knew to stay on his perch and muffle his caws. We all waited and wondered: Would *A Christmas Carol* save us?

I Am Trifled With

Before I relieve your suspense as to the fate of the *Carol,* let me tell you a bit about Christmas in my time. It was not the holiday that it is today.

How do I know this? Like Scrooge in the company of the Ghost of Christmas Yet to Come, I have traveled forward in time. I have seen the dazzling delights of your Christmas. I have seen the cheery greeting cards and stuffed stockings (even for cats and dogs!). I have seen the roasted turkeys and trimmings. I have seen the jolly Santa Claus on every corner, and the fir trees heaped with gifts and strung with colored lights. I have seen the dancing and the eating and the drinking and the merriment. And I have understood one thing well: Christmas in your time belongs to children.

In my time, Christmas was a somber adult affair that marked the birth of Jesus Christ. Making too much merry on this occasion was thought to be crude and disrespectful.

But a new book from Charles Dickens—now there was just cause to celebrate! As he wrote in his introduction, "I have endeavored in this Ghostly Little Book to raise the ghost of an idea, which shall not put my reader out of humor with themselves, with each other, with the season, or with me. May it haunt their houses pleasantly."

And what was this ghost of an idea? It was actually many ideas. First, that it is right and proper for people to take care of one another. Second, that the poor and the ignorant must be fed and clothed and educated with the help of those more fortunate. Third, that holiday cheer and food and drink and gifts and dancing were not just silly pleasures but a celebration of life. And fourth, and perhaps most important of all, that Christmas was a holiday for children.

As the Great Writer said, "For it is good to be children sometimes, and never better than at Christmas, when its mighty Founder was a child Himself."

Within the first four days, the Little Christmas Book sold out its first printing of six thousand copies. It was immediately reprinted, and that edition also sold out quickly. By the fifteenth printing, over forty thousand copies had sold. And, I must tell you, in all the years since it was first published, this one little book has never gone out of print. Do you know what that means? It is a true classic. Writing a classic is the dream of every writer—one that few realize.

Over kippers and toast at the breakfast table, Mr. Dickens pored over reviews of his book in the newspapers. "I do believe the critics understand what I was after in this story!" he crowed happily. "Listen to this."

Eagerly, he read aloud to us: *"Mr. Dickens here has produced a most appropriate Christmas offering and one which, if properly made use of, may yet we hope, lead to some more valuable result . . . than mere amusement."*

The next morning, Dickens singled out this tidbit: *"A tale to make the reader laugh and cry— open his hands, and open his heart to charity even*

toward the uncharitable—wrought up with a thou-
sand minute and tender touches of the true 'Boz'
workmanship—is, indeed, a dainty dish to set before
a King."

Each morning's paper arrived with another fine
review! *"Its composition was prompted by a spirit . . .*
that . . . will not be happy itself till it has done some-
thing toward promoting its growth here. If such spirits
could be multiplied, as the copies of his little book we
doubt not will be . . . what a happy Christmas indeed
should we yet have this 1843!"

But it wasn't just newspapers that praised the
story. Bags of mail landed on our doorstep, filled
with letters. Complete strangers poured out their
hearts to the Great Writer! These good people
confided their worries and misfortunes, bless-
ings and burdens. They told how this simple little
story, as they sat by their hearths and read it aloud,

had awakened in them a spirit of goodwill toward humankind.

The Little Book had found a place in the hearts and homes of the English people. More than a few times, Dickens would shake his head and marvel to me that what had started out as a mere money-making scheme had wound up creating so much righteousness.

Now it was just a question of sitting back and waiting for the money to pour in.

Meanwhile, on the day before Christmas, Dickens took the children to a toy shop in Holborn to buy them presents. Charley chose a set of little soldiers; Mamie, a doll with a china head; Katie, a wooden horse on wheels. And baby Walter got himself a toy drum that he beat upon all day long until the nurse took the sticks away from him.

The Dickens children did not know how lucky

they were! Gifts at Christmastime for the young was not the custom of the time. But it was the custom for Dickens. The wee ones seemed quite happy with their bounty. But by the day after Christmas—what we English call Boxing Day— the amusement had worn off.

The children went in search of a new plaything. And what was it?

I was it.

The Poor Dear, being Heavy with Child, was up in her room resting. Dickens was entertaining a friend in the library. The children snatched me up and bore me off to the nursery.

Knowing I would never bite them, they had their way with me. Katie held me tightly while Mamie pushed my legs into the sleeves of one of Walter's ruffled baby gowns. Then they wrestled me into his bonnet and tied it beneath my chin.

In vain did I rub my head against the carpet and try to pull off the bonnet. Mamie, stern Little Mother that she was, retied the bonnet more snugly.

"Tut-tut, Tiny Tim," said she. "You must look your very best when we go to the Boxing Day party this afternoon."

My humiliation was complete when Charley rolled in Walter's little wicker carriage. He lifted me up and set me inside it on my back (which I hate), tucking a soft blanket around me.

"There!" said Mamie. "Is Tiny Tim ever so pleased and content now?"

That was not the question. The question was, has Greater Offense against Dog's Dignity ever been committed?

The answer was, never!

I waited for my chance, seething in my prison

of lace and linen. When their backs were turned, I leapt from the carriage and, bonnet strings flying, dashed off in search of the Great One.

Save me! I yowled, standing before him in all my ruffled agony.

One look at me and Dickens burst out laughing. His friend joined in.

"Poor Timber!" said he, wiping tears of mirth from his eyes. "They've been trifling with you, have they? Come here and let me end your misery."

The Great Writer returned me to my Natural State. Thoroughly exhausted by my ordeal, I threw myself down on the hearth and slept.

But my recovery was cut rudely short.

In the early afternoon, Dickens set forth with these same naughty children to the house of his dear friend Mrs. Macready. At first, I hung back. I had had excitement enough for one day, thank you very much. But the Great One would not hear of my missing out on the so-called holiday fun.

It was an old-fashioned country dance, after the style of the holiday party thrown by old Fezziwig in *A Christmas Carol*. There were fiddles playing

and dancers dancing. I took one look at the tables
laden with food and was glad I had come.

There was fried sausage wrapped in loin of veal.
There were boiled knuckle of ham and roast shoulder of mutton. There were curried oysters and

fresh herring. There were macaroni, and mashed and brown potatoes, and cauliflower. There were baked rice pudding and apple tart and custard and cold lemon pudding and raspberry jam tartlet.

I could go on but you must trust me. There was food enough for all, including the eager little white dog beneath the table.

I am here to tell you that such dinings, such dancings, such blindman's buffings, such kissing out of the old year and kissing in of the new one, never took place at a party before!

My belly full to bursting, I followed the Great Writer into the next room, where he had lured the children. Bright and jolly as a boy he was that day! Having donned the costume of a magician, Dickens was magnificent.

In a high top hat, he cracked eggs and mixed sugar and fruit and made plum pudding magically appear in the hat when he held it over the fire. He pulled dates and almonds out of a handkerchief! He turned a box full of bran into a guinea pig! The children giggled and cheered. I had my eye trained on the guinea pig when Dickens made it disappear with a poof! Where had it gone? I growled low in my throat.

It was not long after this day that Dickens's third son, Francis Jeffrey, was born. But his joy on this occasion was dampened. Sales of the Little Christmas Book were nowhere near large enough to rescue him from his money woes. Poor dear Dickens!

What now?

THE PINK JAIL

The Great Writer said one morning in the spring of 1844, "I can see no other solution, Timber, my little doggy. The only way I can go on supporting this family is if we move away from London and stay for a while abroad."

What in the world was a broad? I would soon find out.

In July of that year, the last of the *Chuzzlewit* chapters having been written, we set out for this strange new place called Europe. Into a vast but shabby stagecoach the size of Dickens's own library, we all piled one morning: Charles and the Poor Dear; her younger sister Georgina Hogarth; Anne Brown; two nurses; the five children; Dickens's traveling manager, Roche; and myself.

As if all this weren't quite enough of a squeeze, accompanying us as far as Dover were Dickens's friend and his brother Fred.

In my experience, people seem to like being shaken up, rattled, and jostled. Perhaps it keeps them lively and alert. But dogs crave steadiness. And there was none to be had in that crowded, lurching coach. I began the journey cozily enough tucked up into my basket. But things took a rapid turn when the children claimed my basket to store their playthings in. I was passed from lap to lap. When the coach hit a bump, I slid to the floor, where I all but drowned in a churning sea of boots and shoes and bags.

And the noise! The wheels squeaked. The horses tromped. The children whined. The babies squalled. The nurses soothed and scolded. The Poor Dear fretted. Georgy chattered with Anne Brown. And Dickens laughed and sang and offered up plates of food and flagons of drink. He was as joyful and merry, I tell you, as the Ghost of Christmas Present.

Being sick from the motion of the coach, I ate but a few bites only to bring them right back up. Anne Brown had the honor of holding me out the window while I shivered and retched.

When we arrived in Dover, the horses were unhitched and the coach pushed across a ramp and onto the deck of a boat. Dickens commanded that the children and I stay in the coach with the nurses.

He and Roche took the ladies up on deck for the air. As he was leaving, I gave Dickens my most soulful look. In vain did I bark like bricks.

Don't leave me here! Take me with you, I beg of you, good sir!

Any separation from Dickens cut me like a knife, but this cut deeper.

I, Timber—one small white dog—had become lost in the shuffle. And, oh, how I suffered! If you have ever been inside of a rocking stagecoach on board a rocking ship going across a choppy channel, then you can begin to fathom the depths of my misery.

I would like to tell you that life improved when we reached Europe, the land on the other side. But such was far from the case. We were in France, and the French roads were even worse than the English ones. At that time, I was traveling with the luggage

on the top of the carriage. As we banged and clat-
tered along over ruts and stones, I felt dizzy and
sick.

Some time later, we crossed a bridge and entered the city of Paris. Everyone crowded to one

side of the coach to gawp at the sights. I could not stand being knocked about on this coach another moment. I saw my opportunity and leapt from the top of the coach to freedom!

But freedom experienced is seldom as sweet as it is dreamt. There I was, down on the ground, dodging wagon wheels and horse hooves, in a fight for my very life!

Did someone in the coach cry out, "Poor little Timber! He has fallen from the coach!"

Alas, no. Everyone was too busy admiring the sights of Paris.

"*Mon dieu!*" said a man who was crossing the bridge on foot and happened to see me. "Hold up, *monsieur le driver!*" he called to the coachman. "There seems to be a *petit chien* down here who is about to be trampled *sous les pieds. Arrêtez, je vous en prie!*"

The driver stopped the coach with a loud screeching of wheels.

Charley cried out, "Look below!"

Little Katie poked her head out. "Poor Tiny Tim!" she cried.

Dickens frowned down at me. What had become of his beautiful Havana Silk Dog? I lay panting, mired in the dirt and filth of the city of Paris.

"Timber!" he scolded. "You know better than to jump from the roof of a moving stagecoach!"

Dickens would later blame this incident for the sudden mysterious uproar in my bowels. Sad to say, I had poor control over them for the rest of the trip. With a shake-up like that, is it any wonder?

Bad form, Timber! If Grip the Second had been here, he would have said, *Bad form!* And he would have been right.

Bad form, indeed!

Alas, it was not my finest hour.

Then—at long last—we arrived at our seaside destination. It was the Italian town of Albaro, just outside the city of Genoa.

Dickens eyed the big stone house and frowned. "It looks like a pink jail."

We trooped up the weed-cracked walk and into the front hall. The inside of the house was no more pleasant than the outside. It was dark and dank and smelled of mice and mold.

"Ah, well!" said Roche with a shrug. "A much finer villa in Genoa awaits us in three months' time. These Italian summers are so very hot, and you will be glad to be by the sea."

Roche was right. The summer was as hot as blazes, but the cool sea breezes saved us. The children and nurses played on the rocks, exploring tidal pools. Left largely to myself, I dug holes in the sand and rolled on the bodies of dead gulls. It was sheer bliss.

As for Dickens, I have never seen him so relaxed and lazy. He floated on his back in the sea swells. He even grew a mustache! Together, we walked at night when the streets had cooled down. "Soon, Timber, I shall have to get back to work. But not yet, I think."

Dickens's brother Fred came for a visit. He was a fine, jolly fellow who loved to swim almost as much as the Great Writer did. One day, I was frolicking on the rocks with the children. Suddenly, I looked up and saw the Great Writer's curly head bobbing far out at sea.

Dickens! I shrieked. *Come back to me!*

Mamie cried, "Papa has swum too far out. He is drowning!"

"Someone must save Father!" shouted Charley.

With every surge of the tide, Dickens was being carried out farther. Soon he would disappear from view altogether.

Frantic, I started to run back and forth, barking like bricks. *Come back this instant, Dickens!*

Katie began to shriek. Mamie wept. Charley shouted. Georgy and the nurses wrung their hands and cried out like mad creatures. The Poor Dear nearly fainted.

Roche ran down to the beach and spoke with some fishermen who were cleaning their boat. Together, they rowed out to sea to rescue the drowning Writer.

But it was not Dickens they returned with in the boat. It was his brother Fred. And where was Dickens, you ask?

All this time, he had been upstairs in his study, reading. He came down to see what the fuss was about. How he laughed at the looks on our faces!

Welcome home, Dickens, I said, leaping up on him and licking his hands.

But the dangers at sea were as nothing compared to those onshore. And of those, I would be the chief victim.

Fleeing Fleas

I loved Charles Dickens. And I would have followed him to the Ends of the Earth. In fact, I believe that is exactly what I did do that summer. Only the Ends of the Earth could hold such Horrors as visited me.

The Pink Jail, as I have said, was a less than wholesome abode. The fact is that the place was already occupied when we moved in. These tenants were not of the human sort. Nor were they visible to the naked eye. They were, if you have not already guessed, fleas. And they came to call upon me. They were, if you will, my own personal plague.

Why me? Perhaps it helped that I had bathed in salt water and seasoned myself for their greater delectation? Perhaps they liked food with a spicy Cuban flavor?

This is how it came to pass. I was lying one evening stretched out on the balcony next to the Great Writer. He was sitting and watching the sunset. Suddenly, I felt something bite me on the back, just above my tail. I twitched. Then I felt another bite. And another. And another! I yelped. Twisting myself into a knot, I reached back and began to gnaw at the spot with my teeth. But I could not reach the itch. And the itching drove me wild.

"Timber! Whatever has come over you? Did

you have a bad dream?" the Great One asked.

I huffed and shook myself out from head to tail. Perhaps if I just remained cool and calm, the itching would go away.

Taking a deep breath, I settled back down.

And then—there it was again! A sharp pinprick of pain, followed by the most intense itching sensation I have ever felt. The attack, this time, was behind my ear. I lifted my paw and scratched at it. Not only did scratching not offer any relief, but it made the itching worse. My ear was on fire!

"Oh, poor little doggy!" said Dickens, peering closely at me. "Could you possibly be under attack from an army of fleas?"

Good guess, Dickens, I growled. *But what are you going to do about it?*

Moments later, I was aswarm with them.

That night, Dickens wrapped me up in damp

gauze like some ancient mummy. Dickens's theory was this: if my skin was not exposed, perhaps the fleas would leave me in peace. The gauze was most unpleasant. I felt like a side of raw meat stored in a locker. But still, the fleas descended upon me in vast numbers, burrowing beneath the gauze.

The next day, Dickens removed the gauze, thinking that the fleas would be less bold in the daytime. As the children played and the adults relaxed in the shade, I tried to remain calm. After all, why should I inflict my suffering on others? Whenever the fleas attacked me, I would take a jump or two, growl angrily, then return to my place. There I would force myself to lie very still, smothering my sighs.

At one point, it was as if they had lifted me bodily by the hindquarters for the purpose of bearing me off. Well, I was not going without a fight.

I barked at them savagely, racing in circles in an effort to fling them off.

Fleas be gone! I cried.

Dickens lowered his book and gazed down upon me with pity. "Poor dear Timbery. I believe it is his shaggy curls," he said. "The fleas get caught in them as if it were a net. And being caught, they try to bite their way out. I fear there is only one solution, little doggy."

The next day, the groom took me outside and sheared off every last hair on my body. Afterward, I stood shivering in a pile of fur, as naked as a baby bird.

The beautiful Havana Silk Dog was shorn!

Charley and the girls stood around staring at me. They shook their heads in dismay.

"He looks so skinny and sad," said Charley.

"Poor, poor Tiny Tim," Mamie and Katie moaned.

I went off in a corner and whimpered. *Turn away from me, children. I'm hideous!*

Worst of all, I was forbidden to join in the family fun. It was feared that the fleas on my body would leap onto theirs. Only the Great Writer himself risked my company. I think he found it entertaining to watch me in mortal combat with my invisible enemy.

I lay beneath his desk as he wrote a letter to his friend:

"Timber has had every hair upon his body cut off because of the fleas, and he looks like the ghost of a drowned dog come out of a pond after a week or so. It is very awful to see him slide into a room. He knows the change upon him and is always turning round and round to look for himself. I think he'll die of grief."

As my hair began to grow back, he reported to that same friend, "Timber's hair is growing again, so that you can dimly perceive him to be a dog. The fleas only keep three of his legs off the ground now, and he sometimes moves of his own accord towards some place where they don't want to go."

The fact was that, day by day, the fleas had

grown tired of me. Perhaps my ill humor had made my blood bitter and no longer such a delectable feast. By the last week in September, when the family packed up and moved to the new lodgings, I was very nearly recovered, body and soul.

The new villa in Genoa was set on a hillside overlooking the city. It had much to recommend it. For a start, it contained not a single flea. The place was clean and airy, with high ceilings and ancient paintings on the walls. It was surrounded by fruit and olive trees, alive with birds. Most intriguing of all were the two large ponds filled with goldfish. I spent many a day gazing longingly into these ponds. What I wouldn't have given to hold one of those wriggling little fishies in my teeth!

Mamie and Katie kept a sharp eye out. They scolded if I so much as dipped my nose into the water.

The children's days were pleasantly busy. In the morning, there were lessons. Twice a week, a rail-thin man with slicked-back hair came to the house to teach them how to dance. I attended with them.

Although the dance master was not happy to have a dog underfoot, the children insisted.

In the afternoon, Dickens took us to see the marionette shows. When the bad puppet hit the good one over the head with a hammer, the children gasped. I barked. And a good time was had by all.

Through all this, the Great Writer grew increasingly moody. Once again, the supply of money was running low. He needed to write another Christmas Book. His readers were expecting it.

Near the villa was a church whose bells clanged long and loud several times a day and also at the stroke of midnight. It was these bells that gave the Great One the idea for his next Christmas story.

He would call it *The Chimes: A Goblin Story of Some Bells That Rang an Old Year Out and a New Year In.*

THE MOUNTAIN OF FIRE

That fall, the Great Writer had been back and forth from London several times, preparing the publication of *The Chimes* and visiting with friends. The rest of us remained in Italy. While life for the children continued with lessons and games, for me it was not the same. Whenever the Great One was gone, the light went out of my life. I sat around with an aching heart, watching the door and awaiting his return.

To my everlasting joy, he came back in February 1845, buoyed by the success of his second Christmas story. The first thing he did was suggest a trip to the town of Naples. Just above Naples, there was a famous mountain. I had seen mountains before. They were piles of rock that poked up into the sky. Climbing them took great energy and effort. Frankly, I didn't care for them all that much.

But this mountain was different, according to the Great One. This mountain, as he explained to the children, burned and puffed like a smokestack. Why Dickens would want to visit such a place was beyond me. But such was the power of the man that Dickens's enthusiasms became ours.

We trooped from Genoa to Naples. There, we took rooms at an inn in the shadow of the mountain. When we departed from the inn, it was already afternoon. A bit late to be heading out to climb a mountain, you say? Well, the Great Writer had a Plan. The Plan was to be halfway up the mountain when the sun set. By nightfall, when we would arrive at the top, the smoke and fire would be raging.

We set out with six saddle horses, an armed soldier, twenty-two guides, Georgina, the Poor Dear, and the Great Writer. The trek having been deemed dangerous, the children were left at the inn with the nurses. One might argue that I should have been left behind along with them. But I looked so pitiful that Charles softened and grabbed me up at the last moment. I wagged my tail and barked with joy. I would live to regret my eagerness.

It was a beautiful, cloudless day. With me hanging in a snug sack on the Great Writer's back, we started up from the foot of the mountain on horseback. The guides led the way on foot.

Just to make conversation, I asked the horse on whose back I rode, *Do you make this trip often?*

Too often, if you ask me, said the horse with a snort. *It's bad enough when they make us go uphill. But when the hill we're climbing is on fire, it's enough to make a sane horse go starkers.*

You seem like a brave sort. I imagine you get used to it, I said.

Never, said the horse. *Not long ago, a stablemate of mine reared and threw off her rider. Then she ran all the way back home, so frightened was she. After that incident, they let us stop partway up, while the rest of you tourists proceed on foot.*

None of this sounded very promising. Sure enough, before long, a carpet of slick snow covered the trail. We dismounted and walked.

Good luck, said the horse as he dropped his head in a patch of wildflowers. *Tourists!* he muttered.

Georgina and the Poor Dear traveled by litter, sitting in chairs carried on long sticks by four guides each. There was also a fat Englishman traveling with us. It took eight guides to haul his great bulk.

Charles, having freed me from the sack, toiled onward and upward, digging his trusty walking stick into the slope. I followed, hopping from one boot track to the other lest I wallow in the ever-deepening snow. I did not trust the snow. These flakes of whiteness seldom fell in England, so I had little experience with them. Not only were they cold and slippery, but they were also wet. My fur was fine and light, meant for the balmy breezes of Cuba. Here on the mountain, ice clung to it and chilled me to my bones.

Halfway up, we paused to refresh ourselves with drink and cheese and sausage. The nearly full moon had risen in the sky, beaming down upon the Bay of Naples below us. Our group stood in awe of the view while I lay on a blanket, shivering, trying to lick away the ice stuck to my body.

The break over, we continued to plow up the side of the mountain. As the way grew steeper, people began to stumble and fall. More than once, I tumbled backward, head over tail. I would have kept on rolling back down the mountain were it not for one or another of the guides, who stuck out a leg to stay my fall.

Up ahead in the gathering gloom, we saw people who had already climbed to the top earlier, on their way down. Their faces were pale and exhausted. They slipped and slid down past us, disappearing into the darkness below.

One of them stopped, eyes wide and frightened. "It's a terrible sight to behold," he said. "Turn back while you still can! A raging inferno awaits you!"

The Poor Dear looked at Dickens with eyebrows raised, but Dickens only grinned. "What great sport is this?"

"Charles, I fear for our lives," said the Poor Dear.

"It is not too late to go back," said the lead guide.

"Nonsense!" Dickens scoffed. "We've come this far. . . . Let us keep going, by all means."

The means was our feet, and my own four were growing very tired, indeed.

As we neared the mountain's summit, the snow hardened to a glass-like shell of ice. Dickens's stick now became an icebreaker.

Up ahead, fire poured out of the top of the mountain, brightening the night sky and filling the air with smoke. Breathing became painful.

We choked and coughed. Cinders and sparks showered all around us. People staggered and fell. Guides hauled them to their feet. Some fell into piles of glowing cinder. They rose up with clothes smoking.

The moon having been swallowed up by smoke, we were plunged into darkness. In the murk, people argued. The guides shouted to be heard. Fear and confusion reigned. I struggled to keep the Great One in my sights. He was all that stood between me and the inferno that lay ahead.

The ladies and the fat Englishman, still with us, had abandoned the litters and now staggered on.

We stopped to catch our breath on a narrow ledge just below the top. The ladies and the Englishman refused to go a single step farther. Dickens and the head guide and I struggled up the last slope.

How awful it was! The stink of sulfur filled my nose. The smoke stung my eyes and burned my lungs. Ashes and embers lay everywhere, scorching my paw pads. I smelled Dickens's very boot heels smoldering.

Ever so carefully, we edged our way to the tip-top and peered down into the heart of the mountain. We were face to face with the mighty Mount Vesuvius!

Fire and smoke and what looked like a lake of hot boiling oil bubbled inside the mountain.

"The lava level is about a hundred feet higher than it was six weeks ago," the guide shouted to Dickens. "The volcano is going to erupt any day now!"

Dickens laughed carelessly. "Let's hope it will wait until we're back down the mountain."

Dickens dropped onto all fours and crawled

over to the very edge of the crater. On my belly, I
crept after him.

"Do you see that, my brave little doggy?" Dickens asked. "We're peering into the very bowels of
the earth."

I buried my face in Dickens's shoulder and whimpered.

Having satisfied his curiosity, we turned around and slipped back down through the cinders and ashes to the ledge below.

Georgy pointed at me and gasped.

The next thing I knew, Dickens was slapping me all over.

Ouch! I yelped.

At first, I thought I had displeased him. Then I realized my fur had caught fire! Dickens, too, was singed, his suit and coat smoking in places. But the teeth in his face shone white as he grinned and said, "I would not have missed this for the world!"

Me? I would have preferred to stay behind at the inn with the children and the nurses. No matter how badly they trifled with me it could not possibly have compared to this torture.

Normally, it is easier to go downhill than up. But going down Mount Vesuvius was ever so much more difficult than going up. The guides recommended that we slide down. That way, the ashes and snow would gather beneath our feet and break our fall. Instead, we found ourselves in a headlong free fall, tumbling down the steep mountainside without any control.

I looked on in terror as one of the guides, a basket on his head, slid off the mountain and disappeared, screaming into the darkness.

I ran over and stood on the ledge, barking to call him back. But only a stark and gloomy silence greeted me. Sometime later, the lead guide himself plunged head forward into the black night.

Somehow, around midnight, we made it down to the foot of the mountain. The ladies were soot-smudged and weary. Dickens was as pleased as Christmas punch.

When I saw that the two guides had survived their fall down the mountain, I barked to bring this happy fact to Dickens's attention. He, too, was relieved.

"Thank you, my good man," he said to the head guide. "I'd love the pleasure of doing that again someday."

The Poor Dear rolled her eyes. She was thinking exactly what I was thinking:

If you do, you'll be doing it without me, Charles Dickens!

I MEET A REAL HERO

The rest of 1845 was a busy one for the Great
Writer. He penned his third Christmas story, *The
Cricket on the Hearth.* And the Poor Dear presented
him with his sixth child, yet another son. He was
a wee pink bundle with the grand name of Alfred
D'Orsay Tennyson. He was, undoubtedly, a welcome addition to the Dickens clan, but he was still
another mouth to feed!

Money was, as always, in short supply. Understandably, Dickens started to think about writing his next Big Book. Life in England was growing costlier by the day. Dickens therefore decided to take us again to live abroad. And so it was that we traveled to a new country, high in the mountains (none of them on fire, I am pleased to report). The place was called Switzerland.

We moved into the Villa Rosemont in the town of Lausanne. It was a large and airy house set on a grassy hillside above Lake Geneva. I could see right away that the Great One was pleased.

"Timber," he told me as we stood on the sweeping lawn and gazed out at the mountains rising up over the lake, "what a beautiful country this is!"

In letters to his friends, he described to them the sight of the lake by moonlight as "noble." He wrote of the steep up-and-down streets of the town as being like "the streets in dreams." And many was the night, as I napped on the library hearth, when my dreams took me running up and down those narrow up-and-down streets.

At six o'clock sharp every evening, he and I set out together to walk the cornfields and pastures of hay. In the deepening twilight, we strolled through the grapevines in the neighboring vineyard. As we walked, the Great Writer's lips were moving again. He was telling himself the story of the next Big Book. He had already chosen a name for it. It was *Dombey and Son.*

He also began to mull over his new Christmas story. So far, he had only a title. It was *The Battle of Life: A Love Story.* This did not sound very Christmas-like to me. Then again, Dickens seldom sought my approval in creative matters.

Day after day, he stood on the lawn and stared out over the lake. What did he see? Did he see the reflection of the mountains on the lake? Did he see their snow-topped peaks? Did he see the clouds floating over the lake like wisps of my fine silken fur? No, Dickens saw pictures in his mind of *Dombey and Son.*

For Dickens, a Big Book was nothing but a long series of pictures painted in words. How unhappy he was, seeing those pictures in his mind and being unable to put them on paper! For he could not get down to writing until a certain Big Box, containing his writer's tools, arrived from London. The stagecoach had been too full of people and the Box had been sent separately. He waited, in a most prickly state, for its arrival.

At last the Big Box came. Eagerly, I watched him unpack it. First he lifted out a handful of books. Next came a brace of goose-quill pens. Then there was his special bottle of traveling ink, which was built to swivel and never spill. Also there was a bronze statue of dueling frogs, a figurine of a Happy Man with his little dogs (my favorite), and, finally, a carved rabbit perched on a gilt leaf. What would one call these last items? Knickknacks? Good-luck charms? A writer's inspiration? Whatever they were, he needed them as much as he did paper, quills, and ink.

The books he stacked up in a tower at his feet. The quills he sharpened and lined up next to the ink on his blotter. The other precious items he set up on the desk for his eye to rest on when he wasn't writing.

Having finally arranged the desk to his liking, the Great Writer set to work. As always, during the early chapters, I had to remain as motionless as the Happy Man's little dogs. Dickens's concentration was a mighty force—yet it could be delicate.

The slightest movement—the merest sneeze from me—could disrupt his progress. I am a lively and active dog with a rather itchy nose. Keeping still and quiet was no mean feat. One might even say it was a heroic one.

At the end of three months of scratching away at *Dombey,* he rewarded himself, and us, with an adventure.

We traveled, the Poor Dear and Georgy and I (in a cozy sack on the Great Writer's back), by mule upward into a great valley. There was no snow, I am happy to say, for it was September. But the journey was cold and rough all the same.

I feel dizzy, I said to the mule on whose back the Writer and I rode.

That is because we are so high above sea level, said the mule as it plodded ever upward. *The air is thinner up here.*

Do you feel dizzy, too? I asked. I confess I didn't like the idea of scaling such heights on the back of a dizzy mule.

Not I, said the mule. *I'm well used to it. You will be, too, in a few days' time.*

The higher we went, the bleaker our surroundings. For mile after mile, there was nothing growing, nothing stirring. Only rocks below and sky above.

I don't know what it is with my master and mountains, I grumbled. *He loves to climb them. At least this one isn't spewing flames. Still, give me a nice flat surface and I'm a happy dog.*

Mountain or shore, flat terrain or steep, thin air or rich, we go where our masters take us, do we not? said the mule.

That we do, my friend, said I, a little breathlessly.

As we rode, Charles explained to the ladies where it was we were going: "We are traveling to the highest point of the most ancient route through the Western Alps. The ancient Romans built a road here. Napoleon passed through with his army on his way to Italy.

"Straddling a high point in the road is the Great Saint Bernard Hospice. The monastery was founded in 1049. The monks there offer aid and comfort to travelers in this remote and unforgiving place. And it has become famous in the last hundred years for its great Saint Bernard dogs. There, we will spend the night."

I lay dozing, but I snapped awake. Did someone say *dogs*? Were there dogs unfortunate enough to call this forsaken place home? Surely not! This was no place for our kind. There were no birds to watch or squirrels to chase. It was cold and blustery, and the air was thin. I had to pant to catch my breath—and, what was more, I was being carried in a sack like a bunch of turnips.

When we arrived at the monastery, the monks in their long vestments came forth to take our mules and lead them away. They showed us to our rooms and gave us a tour of the monastery. The Great Writer tried to laugh and joke with them, but the monks' faces remained grim and unsmiling.

"A very somber lot, aren't they, these monks?" Dickens whispered in my ear during the tour. "Do you suppose they've taken a Vow of Grimness?"

We ended our tour in a great hall where a fire crackled. I smelled wet wool and sweat. The room was filled with weary travelers like us. But I saw not a single fellow canine. Where were these famous Saint Bernard dogs?

That night, travelers and monks sat together at a long table and ate soup with dark bread and tea sweetened with honey. Dickens shared with me a crust of bread and a rind of Dutch cheese.

Later, in his room, he sat down to write a letter to his friend:

"It is a great hollow on top of a range of dreadful mountains, and in the midst, a black lake, with phantom clouds perpetually stalling over it. The air is so fine, it is difficult to breathe . . . the cold so exquisitely thin and sharp that it is not to be described."

As Dickens wrote, he must have grown weary. His head began to droop. He dropped the quill. His head fell into his arms. Soon, he was snoring.

When, a few moments later, I became aware of Nature Calling, I began to paw at his boot, begging to be taken outside. But he slept on.

The door of our room being open, I trotted down the long hall. A monk in the entryway understood the urgency of my need. He opened the door, and out I went into the night to find relief.

For a moment, I looked around in puzzlement. I panted, my breath making clouds in the air. Something was missing. There were no bushes or trees or lampposts against which a dog in need might lift a weary leg. I wandered off some distance until I found a big rock that suited me.

Having watered the rock nicely, I turned around and trotted back to the monastery.

But the monastery had disappeared! A great, thick fog had moved in. It swirled and danced like a hundred eerie ghosts in a Dickens tale. I spoke up to defend myself but my brick-like bark was all but swallowed up in the damp fog.

The night grew colder. Tiny shards of ice shone

in the air. On I wandered, in search of the monastery. I must have walked for miles. Whether I was making progress or walking in a circle I could not tell. All I knew was that the monastery had disappeared as surely as if Dickens himself had made it vanish with a wave of his magician's hand.

Exhausted and heartsick, I threw myself down on the icy, hard ground, curling up with my nose in my plumed tail. I would have no choice but to wait for the sun to rise and burn off the fog. Meanwhile, the cold grabbed my body and shook it until my bones rattled.

I was in a shivering swoon when I felt hot breath upon my head. I opened my eyes, yelped, and took to my feet.

A Great Slobbering Monster loomed over me!

Don't worry, Little One, I have found you, said the Monster in a voice that was at once gruff and gentle. *How did you come to wander so far from the hospice?*

I spoke through chattering teeth. *I w-w-w-went out to do my evening b-b-b-business, and the f-f-f-fog blew in. I c-c-c-couldn't find my way back. I've never been so c-c-cold!*

Stay awhile, Little One, said the Monster. *Let me warm you first.*

The Monster settled in beside me, and I leaned up against him. He was as toasty as a fireplace fender. In time, my frozen blood began to thaw.

When I had recovered my senses, I said to him, *My name is Timber. I am a Havana Silk Dog. Who and what are you?*

They call me Michel. I am a Saint Bernard. You and I, we were bred for different purposes. You, to be a gentleperson's companion and to live in soft surroundings. I, to be a monk's companion in this harsh place.

My size and fur keep me warm. These big footpads
of mine help me move easily in the deep snow. In the
winter, it falls deeper than the top of the roof.

Remind me never to come here in winter, I said.

Winter is our busiest time. We rescue travelers who

have lost their way in snowstorms or gotten buried in avalanches. We have a special sixth sense that tells us when a body is buried beneath the snow. We mark the spot, and the monks come on skis and dig them out. Then we lie down next to the bodies and warm them as I am doing for you, now. We save many lives. Some call us heroes. But really, we're just doing our jobs.

Oh, but you are *heroes,* I burst out. Suddenly, I felt small and feeble and sad. *Here I had been thinking that I am a hero, keeping company with a Great Writer. But I am nothing compared to you.*

The dog sat up taller and looked thoughtful. *You are the dog who came here with the writer?* he asked.

Yes, his name is Charles Dickens. Where he goes, I go, I said modestly. *To the flea-bitten Italian seaside, up the slope of a smoking volcano, even to a harsh place like this.*

The Saint Bernard nodded wisely. *There was talk this evening among us dogs down in the basement. One of the monks here has read a big book written by this Dickens fellow. It is called* The Pickwick Papers. *Brother Gaston learned the English language while reading this book. It is a truly Great Book, he says.*

Oh, yes! said I. *Dickens wrote that book before my time. But most of the books he has written since then, I flatter myself that I have had some hand—or, rather, paw, if you will excuse the expression—in their creation.*

Well, that settles it. Anyone who helps a writer write books is a hero, as far as I am concerned, said Michel. *Dickens is a Great Writer. Therefore, small as you are, you are a Great Hero.*

When I crept back up to the room, Dickens was still sleeping. He never knew how close his little doggy had come that night to freezing to death on the top of the mountain. But did he really need to know? Perhaps if he had, it would have wound up in one of his stories.

When we left the hospice the next morning, the monks silently led out our saddled and packed mules. As the Great One returned me to my cozy sack, he muttered, "These surly-faced monks are sheer humbug, I tell you."

Perhaps that is so. But this I tell you: there was nothing humbug about their dogs.

A Series of Unfortunate Events

On the way home back to England from Switzerland, we stopped off in Paris. There, Dickens and I
visited the Morgue, where dead bodies lay on dis-
play. After that, we visited the graveyards, where
still more bodies lay buried beneath stone vaults.

You are thinking, what dank and gloomy spots
these were for a man and his dog to visit. But
Dickens had a fascination with death and evil. He
believed that the Evil in life offset the Good, much

as the villains in his stories made the heroes that much more easy to admire.

The fact was, Charles Dickens was a cold-blooded murderer.

You gasp in disbelief. Let me rephrase that. He was not a murderer of living, breathing people. But he liked to kill off characters in his books. It was here, in the Paris Morgue, that he got the idea to kill off a dearly loved character in *Dombey and Son*. Little Paul was the small and defenseless son of a proud rich man. When Dickens first got the idea to make Paul his latest victim, friends urged him to spare the poor child. But Dickens had decided: little Paul must die, just as Little Nell, from another book, had died before him.

When these chapters came out, readers loved the story. They wept oceans of tears over the death of little Paul Dombey. The Great One knew what many writers have discovered before and since. Unhappy stories make for great reading. Happy stories, not nearly so much.

We returned to London that summer. There, Dickens got another brilliant idea. He would bring out all of his Big Books in what he called Cheap Editions, single volumes to which he wrote special introductions. These Cheap Editions, together with the mounting success of *Dombey* and the Christmas stories, began to make Dickens enough money to afford our living in London again.

I sensed, however, that no sooner had we settled down than Charles wanted to pick up and travel again. Sadly, this was impossible. The Poor Dear was once more With Child. And so it was that in the summer of '47, their seventh child was born: Sydney Smith Haldimand—another boy.

Dickens had been working hard. As often

happened, he needed physical activity to balance out the mental toil of writing. One mild summer's day, we took a coach out to the country, to Chertsey, for some horseback riding.

I was not going to ride, of course. Clown dogs ride horses in circus rings, and I was no clown. My role was companion to the Great One. And it was a good thing that I was, because a terrible incident took place on this trip and he wound up needing me more than ever.

Dickens later called it a Silly Accident. It seemed far from silly. To me, it was downright terrifying.

This is how it happened. Dickens was in the stable, getting ready to mount his horse, when a second horse broke loose from its stays. It let out a hideous scream and reared up, hooves churning. With foaming mouth, rolling eye, and gnashing teeth, it fell upon Dickens. It ripped off the sleeve of his coat and shirt, leaving his arm and shoulder gashed and bleeding.

I barked like bricks until the groom came running. When he saw Dickens lying on the floor, he captured the angry beast and shouted for help.

Other men soon came running and bore Dickens off in their arms.

I barked after him, *Dickens, open your eyes. Say something!*

But Dickens remained as stony still and as pale as death.

As usual, I, the small white dog, was lost in the shuffle. So I took it upon myself to remain behind and investigate the causes of this dreadful incident. Dickens's mount still stood in saddle and reins, looking lost. I interviewed him.

What the devil happened here? I demanded to

know. *Mad dogs I have heard of. But mad horses?*

Oh, horses can go quite mad, I assure you, said the steed with a toss of his head. *Everyone thinks summer is a wonderful time for us. The grass is high*

and sweet, and all the world is in full bloom. Farmers turn us out in the fields and let us graze all the live-long day. But among the sweet grasses are weeds, some mildly poisonous, others deadly. Wild mustard and monkshood, deadly nightshade and buttercup. When we eat them by accident, some of these weeds poison us slowly. Others make us go mad. Such was the fate of my paddock-mate. The poor fellow isn't to blame, although I very much fear he will be.

I never learned the fate of that unhappy horse. Dickens's fate was bad enough. He was taken back to London, where a long line of grave and somber doctors came and went. I stood guard by his bed.

The doctors said that had the horse bitten only a little deeper, it would have torn the muscle and ruined the arm. What would have happened then, I shudder to think. Deprived of the ability to hold a pen, the Great Writer might have gone mad.

As he lay abed, Dickens's great head whipped back and forth on the pillow. His fine curls were damp and matted with sweat. I stared up at him, but do not think he even knew who I was. He was overcome with a nervous disorder. He feared that all the villains he had ever brought to life in stories were pouring out of the books to attack him.

To ease his suffering, he sniffed pungent salts and sipped a bitter beverage. At night, terrible dreams plagued him. I crept up onto the bed to fend them off. But what could a small dog do to stop a stampeding herd of Dickensian Nightmares?

When, in time, he was up and about again, I breathed a sigh of relief.

Together, the two of us went down to Brighton, to the seaside, for some peace and quiet. There, Dickens continued to work on *Dombey*. Of the scenes he wrote, one of them described Dombey

Senior being thrown from his horse and kicked senseless. It was inspired by his own harrowing experience at Chertsey. How fortunate he could put this unhappy episode to good use in a story!

Sadly, the misfortunes continued to pile up around Dickens. In 1848, his sister Fanny died following a long illness. Her son, the crippled Harry, would follow her in a matter of months. Many people said that Harry was the model for Tiny Tim, the crippled little boy in *A Christmas Carol.* But Harry's fate was not as happy as Tim's. The Great Writer was sorrowful. He dressed in black and padded about in felt shoes and had the streets outside the house in London spread with straw to muffle the noise of the wagon wheels.

But life did go on.

He toiled at the next holiday book. When *The*

Haunted Man and the Ghost's Bargain was published in December of 1848, it would be the last of the Christmas books.

Through it all, he was pondering a new Big Book. He would call it *David Copperfield*, after its hero. In it, there was a little dog called Jip. Some very foolish people say that, just as Dickens modeled Copperfield on himself, so did I inspire Jip.

CHRISTMAS CRACKERS

The Great Writer had written a good many Big Books before I came along, and was to write a good many more after I had gone. But this book, written during the days of our companionship, was, people say (Dickens himself included), the finest book the Great Man would ever write.

But was I the model for Jip? Bah! Humbug, I tell you!

Jip was a Yappy Little Dog. Knowing me as you

do now, would you call me a Yappy Little Dog?

Jip and I were both small dogs who had been trained by their companions to do pretty tricks. But there the similarity ended. Whereas I was the happy companion of a Great Writer, the Yappy Little Dog (YLD) was the pampered pet of Dora, the spoiled child bride of David Copperfield.

Jip feasted upon lamb chops for breakfast. I will grant you, I ate many a chop in my time. It might interest you to know that back then there was no such thing as Dog Food. Dogs ate People Food. The Dickens family were people who ate increasingly excellent food. Perhaps Excellent Food was the reason why, in the last half of my life—when the Great Writer's career and happiness soared— I gained quite a bit of weight.

Dickens called me Fat. I preferred to think of myself as Pleasingly Plump.

The YLD had his own doghouse. It was an absurd Chinese palace whose bells tinkled merrily when he entered it. It was so big it took up much of the parlor in the quaint little cottage David shared with his beloved Dora. Jip was not overly fond of his palace. His mistress often banished him to it as punishment for his naughtiness. And Jip was often naughty. He barked. He bit. He sulked. He begged. He cared for no one but his mistress.

I was almost never naughty, and my manners were perfect. I had no doghouse to be banished to. Dickens's house was my house. I had my basket, of course, but it was a modest affair, with nary a bell to speak of. The basket being on the topmost bookshelf, where it was increasingly difficult for me to leap, I spent little time in it these days. Mostly, I lay on the floor and worshipped at the feet of the Great Writer.

Dora Copperfield liked to shower the face of the YLD with kisses. Often, she urged David to do likewise. With great reluctance, and only to humor his bride, did David do this. I cannot recall a single instance when Dickens ever kissed me, let alone showered me with them. He had far too much respect for me, and I for him.

In the same year that *Copperfield* came out, 1849, Henry Fielding Dickens was born. (The eighth child! What a prodigious litter!) Charley was away at school by now, but the nursery was as lively a place as ever it was.

When the children heard their father's footstep in the hall, they would run out to greet him, chanting and clapping and beating their fists on the walls. With cheerful cries, they would grab his hands and lead him into their little kingdom. There, they would tack him up for riding, dress him in silly costumes, clamber all over him as if he were a climbing tree, and demand to hear their favorite stories and songs. Surely, there never was such a loving and devoted father as he was!

We went on many seaside jaunts, to Yarmouth and to Brighton. When he brought the family, three coaches were needed to carry the lot of us, the nurses, the toys and books and clothing.

I rode in the coach with Dickens and never again had to suffer the climbing of a mountain or a fall from a stagecoach window. For I was no longer a spry youngster who could spring back quickly from life's heavier blows. When we arrived at the shore, he and I walked up and down the beach. He would stand for hours and watch the waves roll in. Oh, how he loved to listen to the voice of the "hoarse ocean," as he called it.

What was the Hoarse Ocean saying to him?

Was it telling him scenes from *David Copperfield*? It is true that in that great book, the sea—and colorful seagoing people—played a large part. So who is to say that it did not?

We returned to London, where the Great Writer plunged once again into the daily routine of writing. I lay some distance away, dozing and peering out at him from the tops of my eyes. For many months, well into 1850, our lives consisted of writing and walking as he churned out the monthly chapters for his eager readers. And if my legs had begun to tire just a little, from age as much as from carrying extra weight, I dared not let on to Dickens. If he could walk, I could walk.

As the *Copperfield* chapters rolled out, the Poor Dear found herself (not again!) with child. Dora Annie was born. At long last, Dickens had another daughter. How the man rejoiced!

As it turned out, his joy was short-lived. In 1851, Dickens's father passed away. And eight short months after she came into the world, poor little Dora Annie went out of it.

Oh, the grief her parents suffered! After this, the Poor Dear experienced a nervous collapse. Can anyone blame her?

I went up to her room to visit her. I stared up at her, and my eyes told her, *No stalwart female in a kennel ever worked so hard to produce pups.*

"I'm so sad, Tim," she told me. "But I have in mind a project to restore my spirits."

While she recovered, she sat up in her room and worked on a project of her own. A cookery book.

She would call it *What Shall We Have for Dinner?* And in it, she listed all the wonderful meals she had ever prepared for the Great Writer and their family and friends over the years. As so many of these delectable meals had passed through my lips and into my belly, I lauded her effort.

The project (or my enthusiasm) must have cheered her up. In 1852, she gave birth to her tenth—and last—child. Well done, Catherine Hogarth Dickens, you poor, poor Poor Dear!

It was, as you might guess, yet another son. Dickens gave the baby the grand name of Edward Bulwer Lytton. Tossing that aside almost immediately, we dubbed him Plorn. Through it all—death and birth and ailing wife—Dickens toiled on with his great work.

It seemed to me that he produced books almost as quickly and steadily as his mate pushed out babies. Having completed *Copperfield,* that year he commenced yet another Big Book. It was called *Bleak House.*

The Great Writer having come into his own at last, money was plentiful. Dickens moved us into a grand new London home. At Tavistock House, there was room for everybody: children and servants and guests alike. As you might expect, the library was the very finest. There was ample space on the shelves for all of Dickens's books, a generous fireplace, wide doors, and a carpet deep enough for an aging dog to stretch out on.

Life was as good as life gets. Christmas was festive. Charles Dickens, like his creation Mr. Scrooge at the end of *A Christmas Carol,* knew how to keep Christmas well.

On New Year's Eve, the Great Writer gave a Great Party in his grand new home. To it, he invited family, servants, friends, writers, painters, players, newspapermen, and soldiers, people of business and people of leisure. He even pulled poor people off the street to join in the merriment.

There were globes of greenery under which to kiss out the old year and kiss in the new.

A Yule log blazed in the fireplace, where it had been burning since Christmas Eve. Having been carefully chosen by Dickens from the finest tree on his property, it had started with one massive end in the hearth and the other sticking out into the room. With every day of the holiday, I watched as it was swallowed more deeply into the grate. By Twelfth Night, it would be a great pile of ashes.

Gifts were exchanged, and rewards given to servants.

Everyone danced in their holiday finery.

There was negus, a spicy hot punch, to refresh the dancers.

The buffet boasted my favorite dishes: lamb's head and mince; Swiss pudding and charlotte russe; salmon curry and asparagus soup. Young Walter, home from school, tossed potato balls to me when I stood on two legs and begged prettily.

The highlight of the party was a play. As I have said, the Great Writer had more than a little of the Player in him. For this occasion, he built a stage in the back nursery. He called it "the smallest theatre in the world."

He had prepared the play, starred in it, selected the music, and designed the costumes and program. He invited the children, to their great delight, to act in it. Three-year-old Henry tripped about in his gallant knee-high boots and forgot his lines. Even I had a small part. I got up on my hind legs and barked like bricks when Dickens raised his walking stick. The crowd cheered me.

Even though I would live on for two more
Christmases, my final years were calm and rather
uneventful. While the busy hive of the Dickens

household buzzed all around me, I sank into my sunset years.

I breathed my last, in the summer house in France, in July 1854. It was on a day that was as warm as faraway Havana. After I had passed, the children had a dear little funeral march for me. Dickens held forth with a few words in my honor.

In the years to come, he would replace me with other, bigger (one might say grander) dogs. But none of these others meant as much to him as I did. Whether he called me Boz or little doggy or Snittle Timbery, I was the little dog who held pride of place in the heart of the Great Charles Dickens. If that makes me a hero in your eyes, dear reader, then so be it.

The End

And bless us, every one!

APPENDIX

The Man Who Invented Christmas

Charles Dickens didn't really *invent* Christmas as we know it today, but he did bring it back into fashion, where it has remained ever since. No one knows for sure what time of year Christ was born. But we do know that almost three hundred years after the birth of Jesus, early church officials declared mid-winter as being his birthday. This date, around December 25, coincided with the even older pagan custom of celebrating the winter solstice, an event marked by building bonfires, preparing feasts, playing music, and dancing. While Christmas was a time of prayer, it also shared in the fun-filled rites of the solstice. But in the 1600s, as strict Protestant sects rebelled against the Catholic church, celebrating Christmas with anything but solemn prayer and reflection came to be frowned upon. It wasn't until Victorian times that the old pagan customs were reintroduced to Christmas: Yule logs, mistletoe, holly crowns, holiday punch, and Christmas trees.

"People will always tell you that Christmas is not to them what it used to be," Dickens once remarked. He understood the power of nostalgia, a longing for the old ways. Through his many books and stories, Dickens almost single-handedly revived Christmas as a holiday not only steeped in old-fashioned rituals but also to be celebrated by and for children. From *Oliver Twist* to *Great Expectations,* Dickens took a great interest in the lives, thoughts, trials, and suffering of children. He often portrayed Christmas in his books as a time for family and friends to gather together and celebrate in loving harmony. It was also a time for remembering the poor. Dickens's concern for the poor and less fortunate was a driving force in his life and his art. And Christmas was the best time of year, he believed, to appeal to people's sympathy. He set out—through his work—to stir up a new spirit of Christmas.

Dickens launched this campaign with the five Christmas books he published over a period of five years, from 1843 to 1848. In 1850, he founded a magazine called *Household Words,* for which he wrote many of the stories and articles as well as edited the works of others. Every year, he brought out a special Christmas-themed edition featuring holiday stories and essays. In the pages of this special edition, he reflected upon the meaning of Christmas in such essays as "What Christmas Is as We Grow Older." He also invited other famous writers of the day, such as Elizabeth Gaskell and Wilkie Collins, to create Christmas stories of their own. His aim was to create an enduring Christmas tradition, steeped in the old ways but enlightened by social consciousness.

A Christmas Carol was his first and most enduring holiday tale. In it, Scrooge travels back in time with the Ghost of Christmas Past and sees himself as a boy, abandoned by his parents at boarding school over the holidays. Being cut off from the nurturing heart of family life is what turns Scrooge into the cold, tightfisted miser he becomes. By visiting his past, present, and future, he begins to understand the importance of family and tradition and undergoes a rebirth. The new Scrooge is generous to charities, loving of his family, and supportive of Bob Cratchit and his brood, including the crippled Tiny Tim.

When the foreboding Ghost of Christmas Yet to Come reveals to Scrooge that Tiny Tim will die if help is not given, Dickens's message is most powerful. Only the generosity of the rich can rescue the poor. It was his belief that Christmas was not just a time for celebration. It was a time for the fortunate to open their hearts, their homes, and their purses to those less fortunate.

This was not just talk on Dickens's part. In addition to writing about the poor in his books, he was active in many charities. Throughout his career, he wrote newspaper articles and made speeches about inhumane conditions in prisons, factories, orphanages, and poorhouses. His daughter Mamie remembered the Christmas when Dickens opened their home to people off the street. Rich mingled with poor, playing games, partaking of the feast, drinking punch, and dancing.

Today, Christmas is a merry, child-centered holiday. *A Christmas Carol,* in its book form and in countless movies and stage plays, has become as much a part of the season as Santa Claus and reindeer. It serves as a reminder to us, in all the hustle and bustle, that Christmas is not just about buying and getting new things. Christmas is about family tradition and love. It is about remembering those less fortunate and reaching out a helping hand.

For more information about Dickens and Christmas, try this website:

•victorianweb.org/authors/dickens/xmas

Dickens and His Dogs

Dickens was born in Portsmouth, England, in February 1812, where his father worked as a clerk for the navy. During his life, the elder Dickens suffered many financial setbacks. As a child of twelve, Charles had to quit school and go to work while the rest of the family stayed in debtors' prison. His family was eventually freed, but Charles would never forget his experiences as a child living alone in a rooming house and working every day in a warehouse. He vowed never to wind up like his father or let his own children go hungry. He worked very hard and at the age of twenty-one began to publish short stories and sketches in newspapers and magazines.

His first success was the book *The Pickwick Papers,* which came out in 1836, the same year he married Catherine Hogarth. *Oliver Twist* began to come out in monthly installments in 1837. Over the next four decades, while Catherine gave birth to ten children, Dickens wrote a body of work that is unequaled in all the world in size and scope, including *Nicholas Nickleby, The Old Curiosity Shop, Barnaby Rudge, Martin Chuzzlewit, Dombey and Son, David Copperfield, Bleak House, Hard Times, Little Dorrit, A Tale of Two Cities, Great Expectations,* and *Our Mutual Friend.* In addition to these were the so-called Christmas stories: *A Christmas Carol, The Chimes, The Cricket on the Hearth, The Battle of Life,* and *The Haunted Man.* He died in June 1870, leaving *The Mystery of Edwin Drood* unfinished. He was buried in Westminster Abbey.

Dogs played an important role in the life of Charles Dickens. When he was a boy, walking home from the warehouse across Blackfriar's Bridge, he passed a shop. Over the door of the shop was a sign that showed a golden dog licking a golden pot. He developed a deep fondness for this hungry dog, and its image stayed with him for the rest of his life.

When he was thirty years old, while on his first tour of America to promote his books, he received a dog as a gift from an English actor living in Baltimore. This was the Havana Silk Dog that came to be called Timber. Timber lived with Dickens and his growing family in a number of different homes and countries over a period of twelve years. In her fascinating study *The Dog in the Dickensian Imagination,* author Beryl Gray points out that in Dickens's letters this little dog was "sometimes invested with more life and presence than his master accords his wife. Naturally, Catherine is mentioned far more often than Timber, yet for as long as the dog retains his youthful energy, Dickens manages to convey the impression that his company is more fun than hers." It is clear that even though Dickens claimed the dog was "ridiculous," he was extremely fond of Timber.

The dogs Dickens owned later, during his most prosperous years, were Saint Bernards and Newfoundlands and mastiffs, with names like Turk and Sultan and Don. Although he bragged that they were "the terror of the neighborhood," these animals were gentle and beloved by the family. Even though they lived outdoors in kennels, they were Dickens's steadfast walking companions.

One of his favorite dogs was a gift that had been given to his grown-up daughter Mamie. She was a Pomeranian called Mrs. Bouncer. As he had with Timber, Dickens attributed human characteristics to the dog. He found her "preposterously small" yet "assuming great airs" among the huge mastiffs, bloodhounds, Newfoundlands, and Saint Bernards surrounding her. In a letter to his daughter, he wrote, "In my mind's eye, I behold Mrs. Bouncer, still with some traces of anxiety on her

Charles Dickens and his dog Turk

faithful countenance, balancing herself unequally on her forelegs, pricking up her ears with her head on one side, and slightly opening her intellectual nostrils. I send my loving and respectful duty to her."

Throughout his life, Dickens never spoke or wrote as fondly of any dog as he did of Timber, the little white dog who "kept up a good heart." During Timber's time Dickens wrote his most famous and acclaimed work, *David Copperfield*. The first sentence of Timber's story, as it happens, mirrors the first sentence of *David Copperfield*: "Whether I shall turn out to be the hero of my own life, or whether that station will be held by anybody else, these pages must show." Timber was as faithful a companion as any writer could ever ask for.

To find out more about Charles Dickens, go to:
•online-literature.com/dickens

About the Havanese

After Columbus claimed Cuba for Spain in 1492, Spanish settlers arrived on the island with their small companion dogs, the early ancestors of the Bichon. Isolated from other dogs, the breed developed into the Havanese, named for the city of Havana. By the 1800s, Havanese were the darlings of Cuban aristocrats. Visiting Europeans brought these dogs back to England, Spain, and France. Charles Dickens and Queen Victoria, both happy Havanese owners, started a trend. But like all fads, it died out, at the end of the nineteenth century.

Following the Cuban Revolution of 1959, eleven Havanese dogs came to America as the companions of refugees. After this, an effort was made, using these eleven dogs, to reestablish the breed. In 1996, the American Kennel Club officially recognized the Havanese. Today, it is the twenty-fifth most popular dog breed in America, and gaining in popularity every year.

The Havanese stands at eight and a half to eleven and a half inches tall and weighs seven to thirteen pounds. Its coat is long and wavy, thick enough to shield its skin from the harsh rays of the tropical sun. It is a toy dog, but there is nothing delicate about it. It is strong and energetic, with excellent endurance. Gentle and friendly, it makes an ideal companion. So eager is the Havanese to stick by its master that it is sometimes called the Velcro dog. Intelligent and highly trainable, it will often knock itself out clowning around to entertain its human family.

Learn more about Havanese by going here:
•akc.org/dog-breeds/havanese

Owning a Havanese

Most people who live with a Havanese will tell you it is no myth that these dogs are mind readers. Those big brown eyes look up at you and seem to know exactly what you are thinking. The Havanese may enjoy snuggling with its human companion, but it would be a mistake to think of it as a lapdog. The Havanese needs as much daily exercise as a larger dog.

While its coat doesn't shed and its dander does not generally cause allergies, this breed does demand daily brushing and grooming.

The Havanese likes to perch on a shelf or the back of the couch and observe the action. You can splurge on all the puppy toys you like, but a Havanese's favorite plaything is probably going to be paper. Don't be surprised to come home someday and discover that the dog has pulled all the toilet paper off the roll and papered your house like a Halloween imp. Why? Perhaps, like Timber, it is fond of paper. Like any dog, it's best to train a Havanese at an early age to wean the pup off these and other mischievous habits. But watch out! The Havanese is so wily that you may find that *it* is training *you*!

A flying Havanese dog!

Celebrate like the Dickens!

Celebrate the Past

Dickens didn't introduce the Christmas tree. That credit goes to Queen Victoria's German husband, Prince Albert. During Dickens's time, Prince Albert brought the tradition with him from Germany. Today, a trimmed tree is the centerpiece of the holiday. For Dickens, Christmas was a time for fond remembrance of family. Use *your* tree to celebrate Christmas Past. Go through old scrapbooks and photo albums to find photographs of you and your family celebrating Christmases past. With their permission, you can turn these photos into Victorian shadow box ornaments to hang on your tree. Who knows, maybe Mrs. Dickens and her children made a shadow box like this one!

Victorian Shadow Box Ornament

You will need:

Newspaper to protect your work surface

The bottom of a small cardboard box (the kind
    jewelry comes in)

A photograph

A pencil

Scissors

White glue

A hole punch

Glitter

A cotton ball (optional)

A piece of thin ribbon (about three times the
width of your box)

Directions:

1. Spread newspaper to protect your work surface.

2. Place the box on top of the photograph.
Determine where you want to crop the photo
so that it will fit inside the box. Using the box as
your guide, draw a line on the photo where you
want to cut it.

3. With an adult's help, carefully cut the photo along the line.

4. Check to make sure the photo fits inside the box. Trim it to fit, as necessary.

5. Spread glue on the inside bottom of the box and glue the photo inside. Allow to dry.

6. With an adult's help, use a hole punch to punch two holes in the top of the box—one on either side. (You will later string ribbon through these holes to hang your ornament.)

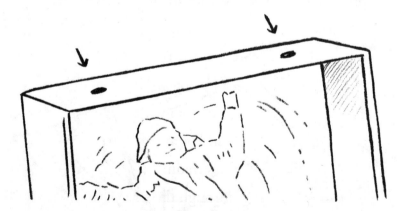

7. Decorate the box using glue and glitter—
or whatever else you'd like. Try paint, ribbon,
sequins, gift wrap, stickers—you name it!

8. To add fake snow to your shadow box, pull
some cotton from a cotton ball and glue it in
front of your photo, if desired.

9. Thread ribbon through the two holes in the
box and tie at the top in a bow.

10. Hang your ornament from your tree and
celebrate Christmas Past! You might want to make
this an annual Christmas tradition, with photos
showing your family through the ages!

Celebrate Friends and Family!

The sweet smells of Christmas are as important as the sights and sounds. Dickens believed in kissing out the old year and kissing in the new. So put on some Christmas carols and, with a grown-up's help, make an old-fashioned pomander, or kissing ball, that's as fragrant as it is decorative. The orange will gradually dry out, but the pomander can still be used year after year, maintaining its wonderful Christmasy scent.

Victorian Pomander Ball

You will need:

Toothpicks

A large, firm orange (unpeeled)

Cloves (probably two jars)

A medium-sized bowl of mixed ground spices:
    cinnamon, ginger, nutmeg, and cardamom

A 12-inch square of tulle (a kind of sheer net
    material available at craft stores)

Two pieces of ribbon

Directions:

1. Use a toothpick to punch a hole in the orange.

2. Push the pointy end of a clove into the orange, leaving the "flower" showing. (As an alternative to using a toothpick, you can put a thimble on your finger and push the cloves directly into the orange.)

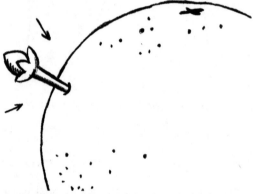

3. Continue doing this until the surface of the orange is covered with cloves.

4. Roll the orange in the bowl of spices, knocking off the excess.

5. Place the orange in the center of the tulle and tie up the sides with a piece of ribbon. (Tie a good secure knot first, then a bow!)

6. Knot a second piece of ribbon to the bow and suspend the ball from the ceiling near your front door. Let the holiday kissing (or hand shaking or hugging or high-fiving) begin!

Yule Log

For Dickens, no holiday season was complete without a huge Yule log burning in the grate from Christmas Eve to Twelfth Night. Try this edible, no-bake Yule log! It's a variation of a classic refrigerator cake. (Your parents and grandparents might remember eating a cake like this when they were young.)

No-Bake Yule Log

You will need:

4 cups whipping cream

3/4 cup unsweetened cocoa powder

1 cup granulated sugar

2 teaspoons vanilla extract

1 9-ounce box of chocolate wafer cookies

2 candy spearmint leaves (optional)

1 red candy-coated chocolate (optional)

Confectioners' sugar for dusting (optional)

Directions:

1. With an adult's help, beat the whipping cream until it begins to thicken. Gradually add the cocoa powder, sugar, and vanilla and continue to beat until stiff peaks form.

2. Spread a spoonful of whipped cream onto each wafer. Stack about ten wafers together and stand them on their side on a flat plate. Continue until you have used all the unbroken wafers. This is the "trunk" of your Yule log.

3. Use the broken wafers (every package has some!) to make one or two "branches" sticking off your trunk. Spread a spoonful of whipped cream on each broken piece, stack them together, and place them on the trunk.

4. Spread a thick layer of whipped cream over the entire cake, and refrigerate for at least four hours.

5. To create "bark": Remove your log from the refrigerator and place it in the freezer for an hour. Remove, then use a fork to gently rake the frozen cream surface to look like the bark of a tree.

6. If desired, decorate with a sprig of "holly" (made from candy spearmint leaves and a red candy-coated chocolate) and/or "snow" (lightly sprinkled confectioners' sugar). Refrigerate until serving.

Negus

At his Christmas parties, Dickens always served negus—a hot spiced punch that made the entire house smell cozy and festive. Make your own yummy negus with some help from a grown-up.

Negus Punch

You will need:

12 whole cloves

3 whole oranges (unpeeled)

6 cups apple cider

1 cinnamon stick

2 cups pineapple or orange juice

4 tablespoons lemon juice

1/4 cup honey

1 teaspoon nutmeg

Directions:

1. With an adult's help, preheat the oven to 350 degrees.

2. Push the cloves into the oranges, and bake them on a cookie sheet for 30 minutes.

3. In a saucepan, over high heat, bring the cider and cinnamon stick to a boil. Reduce the heat and simmer for five minutes, then remove from heat.

4. Stir in the remaining ingredients.

5. Serve hot in a punch bowl, with the spiced oranges floating in it.

Make a Date of It!

At Mrs. Macready's Boxing Day party, Dickens performed magic tricks for the kids. He made dates and almonds appear from a handkerchief. With a grown-up's help, you can make almond candy appear, too, using this healthy recipe for a treat that is older than Christmas itself.

Nutty Dates

You will need:

A knife

Pitted dates (as many as you wish to serve)

Whole shelled almonds (as many as you have
    dates)

Sugar and cinnamon mixture

Directions:

1. With an adult's help, carefully slit open one side of a date.

2. Check to make sure there is no pit inside.

3. Slip an almond inside the date.

4. Seal up the date with your fingers.

5. Roll the stuffed date in the sugar-cinnamon mixture.

6. Serve alongside your Yule log and a steaming bowl of negus, and have yourself a very merry Dickensian Christmas!

Keeping Christmas

Keep Christmas just like Ebenezer Scrooge does at the end of *A Christmas Carol*—honor it in your heart and keep it all the year. Here are ten ways you can keep Christmas all year long.

1. Donate a portion of your allowance to charity.

2. Hold the door open for someone.

3. Write a thank-you note to someone.

4. Set up a lemonade stand or bake sale, and donate the profits to a good cause.

5. Give toys and clothes to people in need.

6. Donate books to a hospital or shelter.

7. Collect food for a local food pantry.

8. Read a book to someone.

9. Make friends with a new kid in class.

10. Above all, be useful. Because, as the Great Writer himself once put it, "No one is useless in the world who lightens the burden of it to anyone else."